# The Climatic
# DEATH
# of Mother Earth

W. Allen

RoseDog Books

PITTSBURGH, PENNSYLVANIA 15238

RoseDog Books
585 Alpha Drive, Suite 103
Pittsburgh, PA 15238
Visit our website at www.rosedogbookstore.com

ISBN: 979-8-89027-282-9
eISBN:979-8-89027-780-0

# *What is the book about?*

The "Death of Mother Earth" is a fictitious tale; about what future promise(s) (consequences) are ahead for Mother Earth and her children; if climatic conditions are not brought under control. As the tale evolves it attempts to elicit your imagination and concern respectively (to peek into the future); an help as many as possible understand for certain; what we do (on our daily journey towards tomorrow) now certainly will have dier impact(s) on the future.

# *Dedication*

"To inspire those of concern an desire a favorable outcome for Mother Earth an her inhabitants; as in now an the future."

## *About the Author*

"About the author!"   I'm a Milwaukeean; an although I graduated from several universities  (MATC a.k.a. MIT, University of Wisconsin Milwaukee,  and Columbia Pacific University). I did not study meteorology! I'm not writing as an expert!  However, I'm writing as one of Mother Earth's concerned children (via this fictitious account); to peek  your interest an in so doing; elicit whatever help you an others of influence are willing to provide;  helping to stave off the gradual head on weather related catastrophic catastrophes;  an their mighty consequence (unimaginable suffering an destruction) may lead.  This fictitious account is a platform  inspired by findings of climatologists and other experts in these matters; including years of personal observations local/national and international weather reports; that include reports of vicious  persistent devastating news of weather extremes; their ecological devastation upon  the  planet  and  its  inhabitants; namely humans who are thought to be culprit(s) of the discord(s). These visitations (sometimes referred to iconic as bombs) of inordinately powerful events manifested in hurricanes, tornadoes windstorms, rain storms, snow storms etc.;  including other weather related events; such as earthquakes, sinkholes, and no doubt the very shifting of the "internal plates" of the earth! As such these warnings are indications, "the weather is changing and becoming more severe with predictable  continued significant  consequences -ahead;  will continue plaguing Mother Earth and her inhabitants. "Unless appropriate  actions are taken; we will continue to be victims; plagued by related suffering an destruction (including as well the violent upheavals of the internal bowels of Mother Earth -an the consequences).

## *Preface*

This fantastic voyage into the future revealing the speculative causes of the dire conditions that will impact mother earth (at that time) an its consequences; as well as our mismanagement leading to horrific consequences.

As the characters and other orators of interest attempt to narrate the story ( possessing limited knowledge and not as experts ) they dabble on, "that Our intentions and mismanagement manifested them/itself in ominous weather patterns; Dominoing mad out of control weather patterns; as the planet's temperature gradually over heated. The impact was the weather and the dominoing effect thereafter ( impacting mobility, harvesting of crops, lives of its inhabitants; as well as violent eruptions and up heavels of the very bowel(s) of the earth -with violent catastrophic consequences).... Needless to say the conditions challenge the behavior of all of its inhabitant; not precluding man mired in strife as he attempts to survive (some of the horrific consequences).

The concern in earnest was a little too late; regarding what they thought was the cause; which appeared to be miss management of the delicate ballet of nature; involving the Green House Gases of the atmosphere that led to; unacceptable levels of carbon dioxide and other Halo products/gases being released into the air/atmosphere; that are/were 'bi products' of many manufacturer(s) throughout the globe; with no political will to stop them. This fantastic voyage into the future reveals the speculative causes of the dire conditions; that plagued our Mother Earth at that time; as well as the consequences of mismanagement; as well as the characters/orators/consumers contributory absent of a positive approach words resolution(s) of the many causal factors (in part may be due to their own ineptness an/or mistrust of their representatives). "Perhaps what really got their attention most disconcertingly of all; was plant life had gradually stopped exchanging carbon dioxide for oxygen subsequently  yielding no edible food; an the poor condition of the soil an atmosphere.

Some of the characters went on to say, "despite the many differences of opinions and influences  agreed it had to end! As there was enough science available (if applied) could arrest the conditions; but here  in lies the rub; as there were those of influence who refused to let it be!  There were samples of an element known as B221 (acquired from previous space  expeditions); when radiated and applied to plant life cause it (plant life)  to regenerate. But, there were those of benefit and influence;   who would gain as  they plotted to secure all traces of the element; and somehow in their scheme wanted to develop it into a monetary system (which would be more effective than what they had at that time); which they also claimed was similar to the old 'gold standard!    It involved the stock/banking system/etc.; whereby they proposed/offered to sell the precious B221 as stock to the public; with a caveat that they could not actually own or sell it. But, they would have a certificate of the same and it would be held in trust.  Also, if somehow they managed to sell the stock the proceeds thereof could not be legally used to curtail the sorrowful  condition(s) of Mother.  Nevertheless, a futuristic space craft/crew mission came to be; to peruse the heavens searching for particular asteroid(s) with at least trace amount of  element B221; that science had previously demonstrated once it was exposed to radiation;  would cause  plant life  to regenerate ( life giving food an exchanging oxygen for carbon dioxide).  Though grudgingly they understood/thought,   "the amounts of carbon dioxide released into the atmosphere;  caused the disruption of the  functioning of "Green House Gases; and subsequent vehement problems (of the conditions of Mother Earth & her inhabitants ); were man-made and had to be dealt with accordingly.

# Table of contents

# CHAPTER ONE



## *Eternity Road*

Fantasize with me, "that once upon a time in the not-too-distant future; as I stood on Eternity Road; with my face erect looking skyward; I could sense/feel our Mother Earth had become very ill!" "Our mother was sick! We've poison our mother. She's literally unable to care/cure herself or feed her children (or other inhabitants either)." "It was as if she was suffering from a very 'viral virus;' brought on by such ailments as factors related to ecological misuse." The "list" of contributing offenders are long! "Where do we start?" "Some manufactures (a significant number in various countries across the globe) an the effects of their polluted bi products; favorable ineffective laws giving them the nod by 'some' politicians; that appear to attack or resolve their undesirable practices. Don't forget ignorance/greed/dysfunctional citizenry; and don't forget just down right 'stupid acting behavior from some' (for it's own sake) -an so on." "There was enough blame to go around! So let us not forget the impact the behavior of consumers contributed (exponentially at what cost)." "The cumulative effects of problems related to nuclear waste storage; unverified control of chemical products; that have leaking into the bowels of the earth for who knows how long (an its effect(s); as well as unrevealed man-made inorganic chemical monstrosities (that very few are aware of); certainly have their place on the list too! "You would think one could certainly conclude they inadvertently contributed to poisoning of earth's soil; which subsequently overtime diminishing her ability to produce nourishing plant life; an the gradual inability of her plants to exchange carbon dioxide for/into life-giving/sustaining oxygen...

The aggregate effects of their cumulative behaviors were -some said, "Mother Earth and her inhabitants were slowly dying from poisoning; secondary to the effects of "polluted bi products;" which were causing calamities on a catastrophic scale never previously experience; such as earthquakes; severe winter and summer conditions; horrific atmospheric conditions that blocked the life stimulating rays of the sun (sustaining less an less life as time passed)."

There were severe storms an floods too!  The end result(s) were devastating humans as well as other living beings!  For many humans it became a matter of survival; or in some  instances outright starvation. While others manage on their meager stores – as they had the foresight to store up.  Coincidentally, it was found under scientific controlled conditions when soil was treated with an element known as B222; it was found soil could be 'say'  reconditioned an able to support plant life. In general the findings were regarded as preliminary at best, as they were thought not to be significant by at least a fraction of the scientific community and citizenry. It was thought more research was needed before  drawing such conclusions. Needless, to say neither was it that believable by the general population. However, as conditions became more critical those opinions shifted/changed.

There  were some extremes! Some died when the government ran low on stockpiles of food and other resources. Farmers and other corporate producers of food were vigorously protective and hid their animals an meager harvest(s). When food was distributed (by the government/churches/nonprofits, and other private entities) sometimes organize flash mobs would appear!  They were often composed of roving  bands of thugs and other desperately needy hungry people. "Chaos and bedlam usually ensued."   It "literally" seemed the nature of all of mother Earth's inhabitants had become predatory.  Mother Earth was certainly dying slowly.

"But, one day she will rise again!" "Just what form 'she' will take –
no one could say."  "Only the future truly knew the answer."  Possibly
it would be without its "number one offender" inhabitant; that appeared
to have cause the mess in the first place – Humans. Some sayed he was
the most dangerous of all species on the planet - or in the universe for
that matter.

Other calamities manifested themselves in various parts of the
world; that included volcanoes belching steam/fire/ brimstone/ lava/etc.
Sometimes there were reports of many horrible fiery huge boulders
being spewed about. "It was as if some angry giant had been disturbed!
Awakened from its much needed sleep and angrily stomping its feet (and
angrily clapping its hands)." "At other times it felt as if it was shaking
this little speck/spear in the universe called earth -with both hands."
"From time to time it seemed as if the very plates of the earth were moving (reportedly, you could feel the results of them rumbling beneath
your feet). Despite those symptoms it seemed as if the planet was desperately trying to selfright/realign itself/cure itself (at least that's what
you might have wanted to think). "Scientists were of the opinion some
continental plate(s) mass were gradually moving." "Other land mass such
as islands/etcetera were moving by centimeters/inches/feet>." Sometime it was as if you could feel "the earth moving underneath your feet."
As if that was not enough there were other times when the sleeping giant
would wake up with a vicious headache and appetite!" During those
times it would swallow up buildings/people/cars/etcetera.  "It seemed
to have had a particular fondness for older gas consuming vehicles/man-
ufacturing facilities/and ther related bi products; that were all known
for their fame for contributing to  air pollution.

"It  seemed as if there was an intelligence in such matters;  as it appeared to Seemingly  consumed many of those items that produced pollution;  that helped to gradually kill her (Mother Earth); and many of
her unsuspecting very naïve  children." Or at times it would just ran-

domly wreak havoc on whatever it could get a hold of. "Nevertheless, it appeared Mother Earth  was trying desperately to self right herself."

The air was acidic! You could taste the acidity on your tongue. Some drinkable water supplies had also become compromised.  There were some reports of  famines in various parts of the earth. The specter of death was all around;  in underdeveloped countries as well as those thought to be "well off"  –at least at one time economically. Some days you could barely see through the haze of  sulfur in the air; caused by what was referred to as "sulfurous clouds;"  that infrequently let the sunshine through.  As a result the ground was usually damp from  what was referred to as "acid rain." The seasonal affective disorder was rampant due to lack of sunshine. Most people never thought about vitamin D supplements to treat the disorder. Plant life appeared confused too as it tried to adapt to a diet of bountiful pollution with its pungent atmosphere and infrequent sunlight; that managed to poke through the clouds.

" Some big corporations/combines and others were involved in producing artificial lite to grow plant life for food.  But, it wasn't enough as there was of course a high demand for any kind of food; as the availability for any kind of food was insufficient; while some groups complained their methods only created more pollution -and not enough food..  Some climatologist argued those methods produced  less pollution. While, others  were of the opinion it produced significantly more pollution."   To some the question then became, "what else can be done?" "Or is this just another Catch 22?"

Truthfully, less food was produce as time/day/months/years went by; from time to time the poisoned atmosphere gradually blocked  usable sunlight; which was  somewhat noticeable as foliage (including trees, grass, etc.) seemed to have been gradually disappearing. Farmers harvest(s) yields were noticeably less; as a contributing result less oxygen was being produced; there was less plant life to convert carbon dioxide into life giving oxygen. To compensate Some governments/individuals/private corporations were supplementing/running machines that produce some oxygen! Nevertheless, the quality of the air was not that great (Just barely passable). Despite these efforts at times the outside air was foul and hardly breathable.

There were unpredictable wild weather extremes! Sometimes it was extremely cold /unbearably hot/ and uncomfortably muggy. At times the humidity was just overwhelming. During the winter months there were unheard of measurable feet of snow fall (almost any where -at random ). Some states recorded unheard of 7 to 24> feet of snow – almost unheard of. "Just plain unreal." Sometimes for extended periods of time there were bone biting chilling subzero weather temperatures; that exceeded past recorded record levels.

There were frequent storms! You name it!  "Fearsome electrical storms, wind storms, acid rain storms, and so on." There were hideous ice storms respectively; as rain turning into ice once it landed on power lines, trees, roofs of homes, streets, etcetera. When water turned to ice in various bodies of water; it made a creepy noise; and also caused rivers/oceans/streams, etcetera to exceed their usual parameters. It was really creepy as it made many eerie/creepy sounds; slithering along taking out people's property; including their lawns/homes/cars/boats/personal effects/legal papers; as well as anything at all in its path – including lives.   "When thaws (as well as other weather extremes) came some opinions; there was a relationship between it an  earthquakes (involving the shifting of platelets of the earth); including landslides, mudslides sinkholes and so on – you name it."

"People were just not used to those severe weather related extremes and other related problems."  During the winter months and sometimes beyond that; highways were frozen over by and icy glaze with a "snort" a la cart! "Snort" may have been a term that originated in Wisconsin; describing a once beautiful snow fall that became speckled with dirt that fell with it from the sky; creating a despicable sight that certainly could not be snow anymore.    It looked as if it was sprinkle with a "diseased black dust;" that was certainly not likely to cause one to associated it with a first fresh snowfall; that you for example would  see on nativity scenes  –on Christmas cards etc.

As a result there were traffic snarls! Vehicles were all over  the place (highways). "There was related untold suffering/ inconvenience/ and invasive coldness and discomfort to the bone.."

Wisconsin was luckier than usual! In the past Wisconsin got its share of cold "discomfortable" weather. But, not to the extent others experienced. By comparison Wisconsin got a heck of a lot less snow/ ice/storms/etc.   But, Wisconsinites did get their share of inclement weather." Out West in California etc., havoc reigned supreme; as it did in other parts of the country and world (as many weather related anomalies were experience)."

In some scenarios people were trapped inside their homes with out essentials. "In other   instances some lost their lives." With the advent of continued  wind, snow, ice, rain, and flooding all over the place; the impact was continued erosion.

Some said,  "erosion culprits all helped create sinkholes; that swallowed cars/ houses/ people/etc. There were also reports of the formation of big craters around the globe; that were  very difficult to explain. Some some situations were such that there was no  possibility of rescue by ordinary efforts/emergency means/ or otherwise.

It seemed as if ice storms fell from the sky; starting out as rain and freezing as it landed on trees; or anyplace else it desired. As a result the cumulative effect of the weight took out powerlines and tree(s) that fell on home(s). With power lines down there was no usable  convenient electricity to turn furnaces on demand via thermostats to heat home(s). However, some heated with gas space heater/oven/or other means. "Warning! Could be dangerous and not recommended." But, what were less dangerous alternatives; that would not result in homelessness secondary to fires; whereby the end result would likely be an increased risk of exposure to the bare elements; and the possible outcome of frostbite or even freezing to death.

Needless, to say the least, "the logistics of travel was just an awful problem throughout (a major nightmare literally all over)!" "Some major interstate highways and tributaries in some instances were (either/or) backed up by traffic snarls caused by snow/wind/storms/floods/ice/ etcetera; resulting in backups (miles of vehicles with no end in sight)." There was much human suffering! Many people needed extrication from there life threating situations;  as some were in dire need of medical attention/hope/ faith/ food/ clothing/ alternative shelter/ and warmth etc. "They were just unprepared."

# CHAPTER TWO



## *Gunpoint*

"In particular doing the season when streets and highways were almost impassable due to unusual amounts of snow and ice; despite the deployment of state troopers/Sheriffs/local police/National Guard/federal agencies/regular Army/ and good Samaritans; there was despicable behavior on the highways and byways; as the stranded sometime picked fights with others secondary to their frustrations; while others attempted to sell what few condiments they possess for ridiculous prices." Civilians were being killed in accidents on highways  and  elsewhere, as they got into ridiculous scrapes; they should have attempted to avoid  –by working together to resolve.  "In a reputed city (not named here); that you may have perhaps  guessed the name of; there were vicious assaults; by gun welding  opportunist –criminals."    "They just vamped  down  on naïve/vulnerable innocent/unsuspecting victim; they had calculated to be vulnerable and were ripe for the pickings."  "In some episodes there were just out and out stickups with firearms or other weapons; including vicious strong armed forcible physical attacks.." Some assailants appeared to take delight as they "mean and viciously" assaulted their victims.

Interestingly enough it seemed that passengers on tour buses, trying to escape,  going here  and there were frequent targets. "These kinds of scenarios (and similar ones) multiplied X number of times throughout the world; just added to the dilemmas that plagued the inhabitants of the world."

As if this was not enough there were "suspect" reports; that there were random  storms where ice balls the size of "killer baseballs" raining down from the skies. It would be just a matter of time before it was just over; if you were accidentally caught by chance or otherwise in one of those vicious killer storms.

In more tropical regions there were frequent than usual monsoon storms, floods, tidal waves, earthquakes, sinkholes, and other related calamities. In other regions of the world there were landslides, mud slides, sinkholes, and so on – you name it.

Volcanoes erupted causing catastrophic explosions contributing to "more" respiratory difficulties.   Resulting microscopic particles from volcanic eruptions increase the difficulty of breathing;  as well as block out warm life giving Sun light; and sometimes resulting in longer colder winters; which further contributed to the dysfunctional chemistry of the earth. There was also what  was often referred to as "vertical lighting!" It would come straight down from the heavens followed by  deafening clatter(s) of thunder. "Bang!" Sometimes the strikes were frequent and  caused many deaths.

There were rumors among rumors; as there were reports of "hi velocity terminal winds"  causing some NYC skyscrapers to sway (more than usual)..   If you watch closely; you could actually see some skyscrapers swaying  -slightly. There was talk about more radioactive plutonium poison –a dangerous biproduct. One can only hypothesize or imagine over time what the global cumulative effect could be; that help create the condition(s) Mother was suffering from.. "Mother Earth! " "She just didn't know what was going on –or what she was doing!" Some said her behavior was instinctive as she attempted to survive!
"As she  shivered/ quaked/ and shook; her backside belched out massive fumes of gase and fires as she raged on for the preservation of her life".

"At striver's row where all ( The good/ bad/ the ugly/rich/ poor/ religious merchants/etc) assembled to buy/sell/ or trade any part or all of what ever they had; they injoyed a precarious peculiarity to Milwaukee (MKE); an other areas across the country attempted to model after it with some success." "Striver's Row!" It was located on North Ave; starting west of the Milwaukee river to Wauwatosa, Wisconsin; where there was unimaginable haggling; as the buzz of the crowd could be heard miles away; while they talked in their best interest(s).     Some of the buzz was about, "the dissipation of the ozone layer which they thought was related to 'Bi products' of manufacturing and consumer behaviors of use and disposal.     Some of the effects were too much methane gas in the upper atmosphere;  that they thought could potentially cause a massive fire or explosion (that could cause a domino effect)." There was talk about the seasonal affective disorder and how it could be treated with vitamin D (or more sunlight etc.).. As they talked you could hear and be assured revenge for some was certainly in the air! With these concerns and others too numerous to mention here; there was a significant amount of division/polarization; that  manifested itself in various forms such as; what was referred to as the carbon tax wars. The principles of the war(s) did not believe they should be taxed or be responsible for the conditions of the heavens, and hired what were referred to as "carbon fighters" to fight their battles;  that they themselves were not able or willing to fight.    The fighters fought among  themselves and other adversaries; who were referred to as the pygmy men/pygmy fighters. There was even disagreement among themselves; as they (carbon fighters and the pygmy  fighters) believe they were all being manipulated;  by powerful radicals and  violent extremists; and some was due to stubbornness/ignorance/stupid acting and down right pigheaded headedness. "They agreed to some extent lobbyists/politicians/interested wealthy parties/ stakeholders/ extremists were culpable.

Some scientists of the globe were of the opinion we were near the end; which was scientifically based; indicating that plants were gradually dying out; and producing less food and/or life-sustaining oxygen. This was further based on the negative impacts on all species (on Terra Firma); including those in the far flung depths of streams/ rivers/ oceans/ etcetera.   Cooperations who had the ability where of the opinion they could produce/manufacture oxygen.  They thought more machines were the answer to produce the oxygen; but, they soon found it was just too big of a job; as there were also related concerns mitigating against them such as: the effects of continued sustained use of fossil fuels;  hydrocarbon(s) resulting from manufacturing of gasoline etc. and its use by consumers; corrupt corporate reluctance to change their methods  of production;  an there was also citizens none acceptance of the facts/observations; as they remained  bound and gagged by denial (and as a result did not demand any solutions).

❊ ❊ ❊ ❊ ❊ ❊ ❊ ❊ ❊ ❊ ❊ ❊ ❊ ❊ ❊ ❊ ❊ ❊ ❊ ❊ ❊ ❊ ❊ ❊ ❊ ❊ ❊ ❊ ❊ ❊ ❊ ❊

# CHAPTER 3

❊ ❊ ❊ ❊ ❊ ❊ ❊ ❊ ❊ ❊ ❊ ❊ ❊ ❊ ❊ ❊ ❊ ❊ ❊ ❊ ❊ ❊ ❊ ❊ ❊ ❊ ❊ ❊ ❊ ❊ ❊ ❊

## *APEX*

If planets could talk they would no doubt ask, "what happened here?" "What happened to Mother Earth?" "How did things go so wrong?" "Didn't just happen overnight!"

"What to do?" " What to do?  "A descriptive history of man's activity on the planet does not necessarily suggest a conscious reciprocating use of the ecosystem in mind; such as a history of planning for discarding/disposal of various types of 'waste' that could potentially be harmful to the environment;  one may honestly concluded there were few well thought out plans involving disposal of waste during the past several centuries (such as controlling bi products from manufacturing and consumption and disposal by consumers). The list certainly would include hydrocarbons an halocarbons  Nuclear waste certainly goes on the list, and don't forget unknown /untold/unreported dangerous "Franken" man-made inorganic chemical compounds etc.  Not to mention leaking nuclear waste in various places around the world. What did it do to contribute to the condition(s) of Mother Earth's " ailments of the soil an plant life demise?"  It would further reveal, "when brought to the attention of responsible  parties; solutions comparatively speaking were at best piecemeal!" "Or just not effective."

The entire process (involving  bi products) could be scientifically documented. Citizens personal responsibility was also  at issue too. "On the other hand some theorists claim,  "there was no real significant sequential cause and effect relationship related to the condition of mother."

The numerous arguments of theorist went on and on. "Classe(s) of them naïvely theorize  conditions of Mother Earth were transitory; and the known four seasons would self regulate and  eventually return for the better -as in the past." Needless to say their theories were thought to be "flawed;"  as they did not take into account continued manufacturing plans to decrease bi products.

"Why/how could others argue it was not the fault of man?"  Can you believe even under these circumstances; some were saying; if you can say man contributed in any way(s); it was miniscule  at best; even if you consider the exacerbating accelerated pace the last hundreds of years brought.     Others argued the contrary! How did things get this far? They felt  it was quite obvious that although man had been on this planet for eons; in pursuit of his own ends; pollution has had an undesirable cumulative effect. Nevertheless, there was still some good shepherds. But, they were overruled – not heard. There seemed to have been an absence of a real culture to avoid such matters. "Consumers were concerned with consuming and producers were concerned with producing."   "At what cost?" It would seem as if in their minds they never thought anything of this magnitude could/would occur. "Did this occur (cumulatively) within the last one hundred years or so? At this point the irony of it all over time could've been avoided/prevented. human has the ability to avoid this  necro apocalyptic cataclysmic calamity. " "But, there just was no cooperation among  them. Period!"

The "Geo physiological internal chemistry " of earth had come to a point, that it was literally impossible to sustain itself!  There was gradually less and less "breathable" oxygen in the air. Some  scientists calculated that pollution had poisoned the earth including its (lense) atmosphere. They also factored in continued use of outdated technology of manufacturing ( yielding dangerous bi products); and the tremendous amount of energy used for transportation/heating/ etcetera.. Of course there was nuclear waste, as well as many other ingredients too numerous to mention here! What  about stored nuclear waste and other chemicals ordinary citizens don't know about?  What effect did it have on the planet; as there was no doubt they had been leaked into the earth for many years; as they literally  changed the DNA of Mother Earth. There were many other carcinogenic poisons as well.  In one way or another these factors created stress on the food chain. It had gotten to a point the harvest for human consumption was, noticeably, gradually decreasing as the seasons and years went by.  It was also noticed that other non-edible plant life was decreasing/disappearing as well.

"In numerous instances some scientists and researchers had found evidence; that had been  debated enough;  suggesting plant life as we've known it will eventually not be able to support life." "Just refusing to yield/not regenerating itself. Refused to yield/budge." "They  (plants) refused to grow." This I guess you might say is the "crux" of the problem!  One could say the solution was simple; as we had the resources to render the problem resolved.  But, such was not the status of the thinking of some of the intelligent life forms (earthlings ) at that time.   While others  further  complicated  matters  with  their  thinking;  the  earth through its behavior would "selfright it self." "How long would that take an at what cost?"

# CHAPTER 4



## *The Crux*

The crux of the problem(s) were numerous! "Hum!" Efficacy was lacking in the government. "It was also thought by some the problems were becoming (honestly) unwieldy. Or in a word not fixable."  "Politicians wanted to get reelected. Selfish influences of lobbyists didn't help either. It was thought by some conditions were 'only' temporary/transitory climatological changes; but there was a complete lack of cooperation from big companies, conglomerates, and others powers of influence, etcetera; who owned or influenced  some companies; where scientist were researching B221;  discovered it had the ability to help reverse some of earth's conditions (namely improving soil conditions and causing plant life to generate life-giving food for its inhabitants)."

In time the planet Earth could have been healed/heading in the right direction; or at least get her off of life support; and overtime there would be a diminution of some of the horrible symptoms aforementioned  -  although she would not be completely  asymptomatic for years to come."

The real rub towards solving the problems was;  some  powerful an influentials were of the opinion; some how B221 could be put on the stock market (a scheme); an manipulated to their own ends. The scheme would further involve;  replacing the  "system we have of printing money;" with a system similar to that of the "old gold standard."

It would be based on B221. Needless to say just to think about this only fueled  more chaos. There in was the real problem! "How to get them to cooperate to ameliorate the proble(s)?" " But, 'some' Diverse groups/people/local municipalities/counties/ state government/ federal government/ etcetera were eventually force to work out some solution(s); to attempt reversing and terminating the dreadful often hellish conditions on earth." There were  solution(s)!  Needless, to say opportunists, corporations, industries, investors, and other strivers, became very interested – as they laid waiting to seek an advantage..

Solving Mother Earth's problem(s) might not have been so difficult!"  But, they conspired (had a dream) to "try" using B221 as a medium of exchange!  You might say, " they got the idea from the so called "old days;" when our monetary  system was based on the gold standard; instead of the practice of just printing more money (not supported by anything)." Their other dream was to put B221 on the stock market; condition upon the buyer holding the stock in name only; which would be retained by a designated company to actually hold the shares; that was further conditioned upon the purchaser(s) of the stock; inability to sell it an obtain actual B221 (or use it or proceeds in any manner whatsoever; in particular  in programs/projects involving improvement of soil conditions; as well as those that would cause plants to regenerate bearing life giving food. The other part of their nightmarish dream was to further (literally) hold the world hostage via developing a mechanism involving stock markets! It would allow them (with out permission or oversight) to manage/manipulate/trade deficits/adjust balance(s) supply and demand situation(s)as well as personal account(s).

"Many were on the fence as they did not believe the scheme would solve their problem(s)!"  Although they "pooh-poohed" it; they had some faith in it too; an the very nature of this polarized hesitation helped the world continue to fall apart around their ears as they persisted.  Unfortunately, "there were many other causes that factored in such as greed an immorality." But, numerous statesmen from around the world spoke against them  (seemingly to no avail).  However, out  of their numbers arose someone who appeared to be fairly representative of their cause; who became very instrumental in the progress that would be made; to eventually cause a craft to be built; that would be used on an expedition to harvest B221 and return it back to earth. As the consortiums/companies/etcetera met from time to time he spoke (frequently); was instrumental in helping to select a crew for the craft; and advice in other related matters. "He was also very instrumental in choosing which companies/resources etc.; that would be involved in building the futuristic spacecraft."

One would wonder why this path wasn't taken a long time ago! Now, seemingly the truth was they (all) were running out of time! Nevertheless, Despite the opposition's position(s); whether they were willing to admit it or not; they were just waiting for word of the astronauts/astrotechs return with B221); and its benefits regardless of how much influence they had. "Ironic!"

Politically (for some) the disclaimer was, "not all politicians were bad (or unhelpful and or corrupt)!" There were those who tried to help; to do their best considering the circumstances." Their constituents never thought about, "once they were elected they would still need the help of other elected officials; to effect any change (promised when campaigning) or pass any law(s)."

Otherwise, "the courts/ government/elected officials/ lobbyists/ etc.; appeared as usual not to be too helpful (in positives ways)!" "Courts rendered ridiculous decisions/orders that caused the holders of B221 or properties thereof; not to turnover any or all of the same; to those involved in any effort(s) to rejuvenate the planet." Otherwise some elected officials purported ridiculous reasons not to pass any helpful laws/orders that would circumvent them. Nevertheless, after the launch of the expedition; it appeared all concerned were anxiously waiting for its return –with their fate..

## CHAPTER 5

### *The Consortium*

It was clear, "the terminal status of mother earth did not occur over-night!" "It was a longtime coming." "In response the government, its armies, departments, the Space Institute, churches, concerned citizens, interested parties, universities, businessmen, corporations, an other Concerned parties (too numerous to generate here); were beset by extreme urgency; that led to their frequent meetings to discuss and planning what to do!" "Out of it all came what to do; to help resolve the dilemma of Mother Earth; by planning another expedition into space to acquire more B221."

There was one might say, "a Consortium was formed; composed of some of the entities previously mentioned; as well as others too numerous to regenerate here -by name(s); that were instrumental in someway to help bring the endeavor of the expedition to conclusion/readiness. They frequently met in the USA, France, England, Japan , China, South .Korea, an other countries. Over time arose a prominent figure who had quite an influence on some of the key decisions!

Most of the resources (military and otherwise) had been squandered /misuse/or otherwise inappropriately used; on everything but addressing the problem(s) of Mother Earth. However, there was a resource/solution privately owned by what was referred to as the Space Institute. It was collectively understood by the consortium; that they would take on the task/responsibility to develop the craft; and bring the entire project to fruition. Nevertheless, there were concerns as many ruminated over what had happened to the B221; that was brought to earth from a previous space expedition!  "Despite the find-ings of scientists  who found; that once  it was subject to radiation;  it seemingly had the ability to say recondition soil; and  cause vegetation (plant life/trees, etc) to grow." However, as previously mention it was not used for that.


"Interestingly!" "Literally Out of the chaos "arose" a figure (Pastor James Deshazer) from Dumas Arkansas!" He was a person  with some health concerns; but was a tireless worker that never took a vacation; who truly made it his business to let others know he believed in God. This was an amazing story within its self.  He also blessed the spacecraft prior to it being launched; and was  instrumental in choosing the space-craft's crew.

He seemed to have had an international appeal.  He was  charis-matic an well known internationally.  He was involved in  world wide ministries an had earned quite a reputation for himself.  Of note was some of his remarkable speeches; as he exalted many pearls of philo-sophical wisdom.  He was fondly remembered for some of his remarks such as: "death is a tragic thing -if you've never lived."  On death that was all around them he remarked, "Nevertheless, you are a mirical! You won't even know you're dead. We live to die (But not like this.);


We must grapple with ourselves to be moral and honest; and listen to the music of the sound of the heart and what it's attempting to tell you; and your powerful peace of mind and soul may come as in a para-dise here on earth; when you finally find and feel/know you are a part of  something  such  (as  helping  others/ministering  to  the  sick/the poor/the 'shutin/as well as the disable etc). It will be eternal -as there will always be a need.  It will give you peace! Peace is powerful and will be your  paradise here on earth.  It may be attained when/where  you find something to be a part of (helping others)  – that may last forever.

He went on to remark, "Mother Earth" is wounded. She has put up with our barbaric behavior, our insensitivities and general lack of awareness an respect much too long.  "But, it seems to appear her conditions had beaten us/all (interested parties)into the realization; that something really had to  be done!  Otherwise, the Homo Sapiens species are headed for imminent extinction." Unfortunately, it most likely will include the collapse of species that we know of   (such as aquatics, amphibians, and those on the coral reefs, as well as all others – we don't know about). The extinction will no doubt be global. Despite this bleak prospect it may not be too late!

Individually and/or collectively we're responsible for the condition(s) of our home/planet.  Beware!  What we think and do  may effect the weather/time/temperature/ as well as other variables; may subsequently have an undesirable unintended cumulative affect/outcome upon our home too!" "Unintended consequences!" "You/we can make a  difference!" Keep the faith, "now that we have brought all representatives (pro) interested parties together to achieve our purpose(s); we've formed a triangle of psychic energy; that will power us through to attainment; and then we can start to render the planet back to the Garden of Eden (it once was) –where love and life can abound."

"Hate /greed/jealousy/our hearts desires and some of our other human emotions have played an expensive part in what we've done." "Do We hate our Mother (Earth)?"  "We must all come together an solve these problem(s); by realizing we are all victims of circumstances; as we were not in control of our inception; what station it may have led to our place(s) in life; our informal and formal education;  our beliefs/etcetera; and realize this as we strive to understand their impacts on our behavior(s) an focus  on doing better to overcome."

The energy to do this comes with our very existence (As we are by instinct tasked to attempt to survive an mastering our environment(s)."Arguable though that may be; there is one thing for certain; if these problem(s) aren't resolved; the inhabitants (past an present) that cumulatively over time has caused this mess to be in the first place; if our home is destroyed; will not be 'back' as a species  upon this earth for eons -if at all." "Who knows what evolutionary path as in physical appearances/adaptiveness/ abilities/ etc) would they be manifested in; that is if they were through a  (paradoxical) evolutionary process of nature returned to the face of the earth – again!" "How would they appear physically?" "Or will we all just perish from a lack of cooperation ?" "leaving the earth peaceful and quiet; as if we were never even here -in the first place?" "Or for that matter never coming back – again."

# CHAPTER 6



## *Consortium Paradox*

Eventually, the  space craft/expedition was lunched after what seemed like eons ago (propelling its self into the vast arms of far/distant "neons" of the  universe). "The task was to retrieve samples of B221 from astroroids -an return them back to earth."  B221 eould not be found on earth except molecular trace quantities; as that contained in an asteroid entering earth's atmosphere would be incinerated (leaving trace amounts).

Once the expedition returned with B221 scientist's plan to "subject" it to test(s) an research(s);  which would also include subjecting it to radiation.! Once its secrets revealed it would be  mass produced an globally distributed . The eventual global application to the soil and plant life would cause them to resume their previous functioning ( respectively as soil and plant life resumed their functioning – as nature intended).

"The desired results would be the exchange between plants an animals!  Plants would produce oxygen an the animals would produce carbon dioxide; 're-consummating' the symbiotic  relationship (as it was intended) between the two; which was greatly needed to sustain/maintain life (with more oxygen an food); and hopefully reveal clues that would help rid  Mother Earth of some of her conditions; that would surely most likely over time lead  back to her good  health."  That is if her inhabitants learned anything from the ways that lead to the lack of function of the soil an plant life dying; an subsequently not regenerating it self; as the two appear to be inseparably related related); an as a result gradually produced less  food or oxygen; mend their ways that could lead  to  sincere focus on the cause(s); that lead  to the vicious horrific conditions of Mother Earth (that resulted knowingly or otherwise from human  use/miss use of its Mother).

In the meantime  court(s) made rulings that were bias; that led to ineffective outcomes; an  one should be warned; the following opinions of these fictional characters created on the following pages;  may not be helpful either; an not intended for one to base an opinion on (in particular) about what had caused the dire condition(s) of mother earth; or for that matter how to remedy them.   Otherwise, the best course of action may be researching the matter yourself; and consultation(s) with experts in the matter; before drawing any conclusions about what you and others can do to address future causative challenges.

Some of the concerned ones attempted to point out; it was just not renewing the relationship between humans an plants (exchanging co2 for o2); that explained the condition(s) of Mother Earth -at that time! "The mysteries remained!"  For example what was causing the upheavals of earth; an what  specifically had caused the soil and plant life to malfunction." We know that carbon dioxide an oxygen respectfully are also produced from other sources -on earth!   Ironically, the amounts of carbon dioxide that's emitted in exchange for oxygen; for human consumption (an other animal life);  one could say were at a critical balance;  but, were   not   necessarily   the   culprit(s);   that   interfered   with   the purpose/function of greenhouse gasses (GHG) in the atmosphere.

"They also expressed  concerns about the ability of those greenhouse gases (GHG) to help regulate the average temperature of earth (as intended by nature); as the vast majority of anthropogenic carbon dioxide emissions (that interfere with the function of GHG) came from combustion of fossil fuels (primarily coal, petroleum, including oil) and natural gas; with additional contributions from cement manufacturing;

fertilizer production; deforestation and other uses of the land." "They also noted co2 is released into the atmosphere when Volcanos  erupt; which contribute to blocking out of infra rays of the sun." They also mentioned they heard there were theories about, "treating excessive CO2 in the  oceans and atmosphere (involving mixing of CO2 with magnesium hydroxide and burying the excess of it underground or in oceans)."  "Excessive CO2 underground or in the oceans?)."  "The orators were also careful to point out they were not sure about what had been  mention; as it was their understanding of the information on the subject(s); they had been  exposed to; may not have been completely accurate." Nevertheless, they went on to mention the effects of man  made Chlorofluorocarbons (CFCs), Hydrofluorocarbons  (HFCs),  an Per-fluorocarbons (CF4, C2F6)!   Halocarbons (fluorocarbons aerosols) may also help to destroy stratospheric ozone.

As if that was not enough to process; they also tried to point out as best they could;

that the manufacturing process(s);  that converts non-methane volatile or ganic compounds (NMVOC)  into Carbon dioxide; could also lead to functional interference with tropospheric ozone. "Examples of some of these NMVOC(s) may include a large variety  of chemically different  compounds (such as benzene, ethanol, formaldehyde,  cyclohexane, 1,1,1-trichloroethane,  acetone and other fluorocarbons) have an effect;  as they may also destroy stratospheric ozone; which protect us (from to  much of the sun's ultra violet rays).

"There appeared to be no scientific doubt they've interfered with the functions of GHG (like a delicate ballet); that has been cumulatively interfered with over time; has eventually caused unintended devastating consequences; for Mother Earth and her children."

They also mention, "On the other hand 02 (Oxygen) is a colorless tasteless odorless gaseous element found in  water/rocks/minerals/ and many other organic compounds;  with the ability to combining with almost all elements.  But, will not combine/bond with inert gases an is not a significant factor in the functioning of GHG.

Some of the orators caution that one should keep in mind; the explanations about carbon  dioxide an oxygen do not directly explain the disastrous condition Mother Earth founded  herself in; as they were not purporting "themselves" to be experts in  such matter(s). But, were attempting to share information they had gotten from others (experts/media/pros/cons/ etc.);  an as such were not responsible for the accuracy of the same –or otherwise.

But, rather attempting to explain their objective(s)  were to let them know; they "now" understood how they might have interpreted what was streaming about the conditions; the complexities of it upon their feelings; an  how the information presented to them could have been cognitively processed;  which were the basis for their subsequent choices; that  sometimes manifested itself in undesirable negative violent behavior (results);  that did not directly address the problems of Mother Earth (or their survival of  those dreaded times).

They went on to say, "However,  as we enlist your support;   we want you to know;  we are  here for you; to help turn around these horrific conditions we find ourselves in on this planet."

For better or worse for insight/education about the mater,  "some recommended (if they were interested in GHG/climate change/etc.) to further understand the behavior(s)/relationship(s)  of  the effects of the vast majority of anthropogenic carbon dioxide emissions; which   come from human usage; such as combustion of fossil fuels produces harmful amounts of carbon dioxide; that interacts w/  GHG, etc.  One should also concern themselves with some knowledge regarding/about the effects of green house gasses an how they work (having to do with regulating  earth's temperature an how it effects  human's)."  "The process is consummated primarily with gasses (GHG) in Earth's atmosphere with such as  water vapor (H2O), carbon dioxide (CO2), methane (CH4), nitrous oxide (N20), an  ozone (O3).”  “Without them the mean/average temperature on earth would be about -18°C (0°F) instead of the current average of 15°C (59°F).”

“Adding  further confusion to the dilemma(s) some mention, “Soot!”  “Another culprit?” They mention  “Soot” was literally a mass of impure carbon particles in the atmosphere (existing in  a solid or liquid state(s);  caused by incomplete combustion of hydrocarbons (sounds familiar?)!  “These  airborne contaminants (Soot)  are  derivatives of pyrolysis’s incompletely  burning of product(s) such as gasoline, trash, wood, cooking, as well as forest fires  –just to name a few of those products.”  This list (by no means conclusive) also include  various material used in manufacturing processes.  It may also be associated with Acid Rain,  exhaust from diesel products,  an malfunctioning of Ozone. They also noted, “those airborne contaminants impact the climate , human  health (including respiratory ailments), and various types of cancers (including lung cancer)...

They further purported (again) to their hearers,  “they were not experts in the those matters; and the information was not intended to be the equivalent of a lesson; a refresher course;  or preparing them for a pop quiz.”  Most of the speakers had “alternative” motives; an readily admitted they were  not sure; if the information was correct or not; as it was only what they had heard; an read and thought they understood. “They wanted to let them know they had their best interests in  mind (to work with them and to help them understand what was going on an help solve their problems);  and let them know they understood; how extremely hard an dangerously complicated it must have been; to have made  decisions based upon  their circumstances ( which were based upon what was thought to have caused the dire conditions of Mother Earth).”

But, for better or worse they advised them to pursue the matter first hand; ask  questions of those who were thought to be qualified to answer their concerns; an in their pursuit they may  find of interest if not entertaining; some climatologists /scientist/etc/ based upon  their research an studies; had concluded the earth is a living organism; an that the surrounding atmosphere is  "like blanket surrounding Mother Earth!" Comparatively speaking the theory is, "its (the blanket) function is  liken to "Bio" breathing apparatus;  sustaining life on the planet."  Forlorn as the speaking event(s) were; some went away with a further understanding of the cause(s); and others were still haunted by the notion; even though  GHG were thought to have  specific functions in the matter;  anthropogenic carbon dioxide  emissions etcetera also caused by humans; and  cumulatively over time creating a disturbance in that delicate ballet of balance;   causing a GHG effect interfering with the temp; leading to correspondingly related horiffic weather conditions; that at times further manifest themselves into deadly frightful upheavels from  the bowels of the earth; that  further manifested itself with challenging difficulties  for its inhabitants.

They also added, "the lesson(s) for the future appeared to be in their hands;  an that they must get a further academic understanding of the challenges; as they knew it was within  their powers; to do their part to gradually decrease; and prevent future calamities; as they attempted to restore Mother to her once healthy condition."


"But, just what caused the over all mal conditions of Mother Earth; maybe some what of a mystery or an overt undeniable truth!"  Some sayed (with radiant ignorance) it was caused by the "green house gang (GHG);" that they the "greenhouse gas gang" were causing horrific weather conditions (such as storms, etcetera affected the earth internally too; manifesting itself in Mother Earth's stomach and bowel's discomfort and upheavals (resulting in symptoms such as sink holes/earth quakes/ volcanic eruptions eruptions/ tremors , an so on).  Others blamed bi products of manufacturers; while others blamed consumers for their chronic careless habits of consumption/disposal – an overall misuse of their mother's  (environment). Don't forget stored atomic waste (may be leaking into the bowels of the earth) in various parts of the world; and doing that process may involve dangerous bi products too.    There are also unspoken invisible cursed horrific inorganic chemical monsters; created by private industry too; that we will never know about or their name(s); let alone their effect on  Mother Earth an its inhabitants."

Again,  the irony was; "there was B221 on earth; brought back from a previous space expedition."     But, as previously mentioned, "there lies the rub/scheme/scam/etc!"   There  were those of influence who sought to use it for their own selfish ends! Namely, "Use it to establish a scheme that they thought would work for them; as they would use the valuable B221 to create a monetary standard/system (which involve the stock markets etc.)

"In the mean time; whenever the sleeping Giant was once again awaken; it would  indiscriminately wreak more havoc on Mother Earth and its inhabitants."   There were weather reports of storms that were characterized as a  haunting sickly looking foggy "atmospheric" green in appearance. Meteorologist explained the color/phenomena as having to do meteorological with atmospheric conditions (involving in particu-lar clouds and bending of sun rays ); as the sunrays are being bent by the moister in the clouds; producing that  effect; was thought by many to be the cause of those frightening hellish storms; which in all prob-ability did not explain the sickly looking foggy appearances (or the storms for that matter).    Being in the right place at the right time as sunrays attempt to penetrated the clouds to cause the green color effect – was not the entire explanation.  It was much more involved  than  that. Once you were ever inside of such a storm; it was as if all of the elements were upon you. The most frightening was the size of the hailstones that could rain down upon you (if you were unfortunate enough to be in such a storm).   "Otherwise, it encompassed many blinding miles."   It essentially was a storm that you would've been advised not to attempt traveling through ; as the visibility would be zero;  and if you were unfortunate enough not to be able to find shelter; hail the size of golf balls would raining down upon you; an in all probability you would become one of its  fatal statistics/ victim(s)..  Seeking shelter in your automobile (but only as a last resort) was not recommended; as its effects upon you would be devastating (as you would be severely bludgeon which would no  doubt lead severe life-threatening injuries or loss of your life – being the end result). In fact your car should be sheltered too;  as the windows, various components, an soft sheet metal body skin/covering in some cases would literally be destroyed...

And of course there were some reports  that were surely suspect; as it was claimed blocks of ice also fell from the sky, that appeared to weight at least 25 lbs.  However, There was never a verifiable case! The claims were suspect; as they were usually reported as being "cubical" in shape; and crushed into many pieces upon impact.   "Nevertheless, the sentiment was heaven help you -if you ever became a victim." If in fact this was true, "it ment instant death leaving a very unpleasant sight."

This phenomena was not really new; as in the past there were reports of similar storms.  But, not with hail an or ice a La mode.  There were many meteorological reports! Their appearance(s) was really unpredictable.  There were reports of similar storms in arid  desert(s); where vicious sand storms were such; that you couldn't see you hands in front of your face. Instead of hail an its effects upon you;  there was the razor's edge of sand seemingly at the hands of a madman -cutting all it touched.  During those particular storms they were not accompanied by the foreboding frightening green color!" There was just razor cutting sand that also blotted out the sky an your vision -if you dared to look" . In either event, it was strongly advised to avoid those area(s) or seek shelter immediately...

No one really knew how long it would take the Witchcraft to return! Nor could they have imagined what the crew must have seen on their journey back to earth!  "The sky an the beautiful snow white clouds had all but disappeared (into various tell tale mixtures of colors of puking yellow/green/dark gray colors)." The polar snow white caps were also presenting in a similar uninviting disarray of colors. It was a foreboding looking quarantined planet; appearing as a sickly yellowish green scabbed over sore(s); bounded by inertia as it loomed along in space; as a curious neighbor (an on lookier -the moon) could not have help but wonder in amazement, "What's happening to mother earth?" "Am I in the wrong orbit or what?"

"When the expedition returns with B221; its secrets will be laid bare/learned an mass-produced; through various international programs; an would be applied throughout the lands of the globe. Its expectations/ hopes over time would be infectiously effective; as it corrects whatever caused the breakdown of the symbiotic relationship; involving the exchange of carbon dioxide from humans in exchange for oxygen from plants. "Not to mention plants (that died or were dying ) would start to gradually produce edible food." That would indeed be a blessing involving the restoration of plant's ability to produce food too. But, the gradual dying out of plants and their inability to produce food was just another part of the mysterious riddle; an not a panacea to cure/correct all of Mother Earth's previously mentioned devastating other ills of cataclysmic proportions; as there was a menu of conditions that could not be addressed alone by B221.. It was a complicated menu involving many horrible earth bound problems; as well as many theories that caused the conditions of mother Earth. For example as previously mentioned some speakers who had an opportunity to speak; believed that greenhouse gases were the cause/ Genesis of the plight of mother Earth's horrific problems; (including the exchange between plants and animals of carbon dioxide and oxygen); and contrary to that there were others who did not believe the same. Although, they expressed what they thought/believed was true; it only complicated matters; causing mass confusion for their constituents and others...

"Others were of the opinion green house gases protected earth by attempting to regulate its average temperature; allowing sunrays in; an or allowing the build up heat to escape into the atmosphere - when appropriate."   They also disclose that they were not climatologists or experts in such matter(s); but that they may be a little mixed up too; an not really trying to completely explain the phenomenon(s) as such (with 100% accuracy).

But, rather their purpose was attempting to explain/talk about it in such away as to convey to them how they felt; an how it influenced their choices of behaviors (for better or worst). They wanted to be clear about the extent of what they knew; about what  green house gases and  their effects. "Or, for that matter how or if it was related to the poisoning of the soil and vegetation; and what role that may have also played in the upheaval of the bowels of the earth;  that also helped to cause the  horrible conditions -that plagued Mother Earth.

Interestingly, there were few accusations about the effect of global manufacturing bi products and their contributions! However, of interest were spokesmen who spoke about;  the concept of "carbon storage;" that would help solve some of the ills of mother Earth.   They explained, "greenhouse gases (specifically carbon dioxide) an 'over overabundant bi product' from the use of fossil fuels too; which appeared to have had the ability to set off the delicate  balance of greenhouse gases (ability to regulation); could be capture and stored underground in rocks  (there were also theories about it being stored in oceans) indefinitely;  that could be a genesis to help rout the horrible conditions of Mother Earth (and suffering of its inhabitants)." But,, "Needless to say further  confusion and apprehension continued to blanket many spectators."

"I'm sure wiser ones could postulate what may have caused the ruin-
ation of the soil and plants (including the other horrific challenging conditions that plagued Mother Earth) and leave it at that!"     However,
they did warned and suggested, "we all should do our part to educate
ourselves/exert our influence(s);   to minimize the deleterious effects of
too much menacing human made gases (etcetera); that had significantly
disturb the delicate balance (the ballet)  of the function of greenhouse
gases (etcetera)."

# CHAPTER 7



## *The Crew*

The space Institute (nonprofit) and other resources to numerous to mention worked collaboratively with "Bryce an Lauryn" (with their futuristic ideas). There was also a cadre of engineers/scientists/acquaintances that worked with them; to produce the very futuristic spacecraft (dubbed the Witch Craft); that would get the challenging job done! It was a very able futuristic spacecraft with many built in abilities with great promise(s).

Bryce was thought of as a very brilliant individual with a touch of savant (abilities). He was a young man with a magnetic personality and was usually able to get along with everyone. His crew members had attended the same university – an they often exchange ideas. Sometimes , they discuss how Mother Earth had gotten into her condition; with her continued rapid deterioration; involving the planet literally stop growing plant life; and thereby producing less oxygen. His desire seemed to have been to solve the "neons" of the universe – derived from astrological studies. But, he became focused on a particular theory after stumbling upon a student's work at the University Wisconsin –Milwaukee. It theorized that gravity/gravitational forces throughout the universe could be harnessed – to power motors. The concept of this type of motor would not be as we've know them to be. It would involve several motors working together as one; including numerous powered gyroscopes and strategically use magnets. Nuclear power would also be involved giving it literally an inexhaustible ability to travel throughout space.

There were many obstacles an riddles that had to be solved.  For example it was though by some; the "Van Allen radiation belt" could disrupt functioning of the on board computers; which could result in the loss of guidance by the craft.  In event of this occurring an override was  built into the safety system would correct its course.

There were problems with their electromagnetic pulse generator(s); an nanotechnology   engineering elements and its limits etcetera;  an they could not  academically completely describe how the motors of the witchcraft interacted with the various electromagnetic waves of the universe; as they had their many difference/opinion(s);  nevertheless, they did agree the "Witch Craft" would be more than capable of completing it's anticipated mission.

The witchcraft presented itself as a foreboding compacted black piece of metal; shaped like a saucer (shaped to accommodate on board gyroscopic/huge magnets/ and other motors); hoovering a foot or so above the surface of the earth.   Near the top of the craft were several small  windshield shaped like Windows.  Near the bottom of the craft were circular shaped white lights; that revolved around the craft.  There were several universal lights (two aft and two astern -respectively).  .

Ironically,  "as the various crews/ workmen/ scientists/etcetera worked to complete the craft; its ominous appearance seemed to have inspired them to accomplish their many tasks;  as well  as growth in their confidence; it would really be capable of travelling into the vastness of space and completing the mission. The presence of the ominous black shaped  craft seemed to have inspired them  as they installed  reliable challenging super high-tech  avionics/etc.; and other on board futuristic abilities."  There were many built in fail safe devices! Of interest was, "in the event of an impending unanticipated disaster; the auto  pilot system would launch a 'miniature rocket propelled craft;' capable of returning a payload of B221  back to earth -assuming the payload  had previously been loaded into the rocket."

"Lauryn (PHD) the pilot was a very stable and cool entity; not usually rattled by details!" She was aware of constantly changing environmental conditions; an responding accordingly as needed. She had a wide dearth of education/experience/competencies and extensive trained for the mission.

Some of her colleagues described her/background; as an expertise involved controlling devices by "thought; based upon the science/research/experimentation of the utility/application of the Alpha Brain Wave (usually produced when relaxed or calm) of humans. "As the neuron(s) in the brain communicate they it produce five distinct measurably different electrical waves/impulses (referred to as Delta/Theta/Alpha/bata/Gama). This activity can be measured! The Alpha Wave produce an oscillation range of 8hz to 12 hz (cycles per second). They can also be observed via an EEG or electroencephalograph. The science/study/ an experimentation with the Alpha Wave is not new; as its discovery dates back at least a century or more past. Some of its applications were instrumental in diagnosing/treatment/control of seizure disorder(s). Other directions as in engineering involved adapting the Alpha Wave to a computer interface; which demonstrated proof physical objects could be moved. Since then its use has evolved into more sophisticated levels of application(s); to control cars/airplanes/etcetera (which is one of Lauryn;s specialty/expertise(s)... With the aid of "Reese" her very competent assistant/aid, an understudy assisted in the installation some of the technology into the Witch Craft; giving the pilot the ability to control the craft's guidance system; with out any hands on the control panel. This technology not to be taken "lightly" involved many hours of training; to become proficient/competent to pilot such a Say Craft. However, the above explanation regarding the Wave maybe overly simplified; as the description(s) were only intended to be general; and articulated as a thought how they understood it (about the pilot and conceptual use of the Alpha Wave); an its applications (any further knowledge must be sought).

The third crew member also received extensive training for the mission. "Of the crew he  may have been the most interesting!" He was a genius. A trained nuclear botanist and  involved in various discoveries; involving  other abilities of B221; an he also agreed with other scientists (that B221 would be therapeutic an help the dying planet rejuvenate itself). He believe in order to reach the level of efficacy needed, "the atmosphere would have to be cleansed;  allowing bi mobility of sunlight rays; would take approximately five years." As a caveat at least on one occasion he reputedly had been heard to have said, "and of course offenders (should be marooned on an island).  Other Particularly non-compliant  manufacturers/consumers/ politicians/ etcetera would have to modify their behaviors to d/c pollution bi product(s) etc.; which would involve a higher standard/level of participation going forward in order to be effective."

"He was also concerned about anatomical weights of planets; as he theorized planets were of approximate/appropriate weight(s)/size(s)/orbiting speed(s)  (for a purpose) to keep them in their orbit(s); and if there was any significant change(s);  they could lose their stabilizing factor(s) of inertia; and gravitationally drawn into the sun."  His theory was based upon  man's ever-growing  thoughts and  desire to mine other planets; an what he theorized could be the end results; as in the future when he (man) could hop/skipped/jump over planet(s); exploring for precious metals to mine/etcetera (including his own planet Earth);  which could lead to a significant degrading; that could compromise their metric tonnage/weights etc.; and conceivably eventually drawing them into the sun or elsewhere -causing horriffic consequences.  "He also verbalized cringing thoughts of earth being drawn into the black hole of space/disappearing into antimatter/or elsewhere; or their could also be far more reaching painful undesirable consequences."  His warning was, "not to tamper with the fragile metrics of the planet(s); as it could conceivably destabilize the rest of the solar system." Some retorted, "why don't we just moved to another planet; or atlease consider moving before that occurred?" He was against that basically because, "the one they lived on was not being managed -as needed."

He was Also noted for his work on developing what was referred to as a versatile "Universal Sonic Weapon! " An of course it was touted as being the weapon to end all war(s) an usher in peace to all mankind. The weapon known for its range an potentially horrific destructive powers. It could also (theoretically) shoot nuclear waste materials into space; where it could either be drawn into the sun or "other parts of the universe" or even another planet; and could conceivably help mine valuable metals from other planet(s)... Although, its use was not practical at that time; it was a prototype of what was to come.

As it was developed its destructive power could be metrically managed to determine the range of motality on humans (civilians); as well as the range and level of destruction on battlefield(s). Its potential for destruction was unlimited; as it could destroy our disable battlefields/battleships/airplanes/satellites/communication equipment/etcetera. Of course buildings and dense populations could be targeted as well. Nevertheless, critics were of the opinion, "it was a hideous weapon an would fail; to end all wars and bringing peace to all mankind; as other past promising weapons had; an furthermore would lead to the distruction of mankind."

The forth member of the crew's team would not be on board during the mission! He was an army General/the director/ chief engineer/ ramrod/etectera responsible for the success of the entire mission; that also included responsible management of the support team(s).. His background involved several degrees in various "related" areas of engineering. He would have the last word to approve

launch of the "WitchCraft" into space.   Otherwise, he was a very interesting character with  lots of theories! One of his theories of interest; which was similar to one previously mentioned was; "he
postulated Mother Earth was really comparatively speaking part of a
neuron in a huge brain; that was malfunctioning  manifested in symptoms mentioned above –causing havoc."

"She was thought to be (in the scheme of the universe) just a little
malfunctioning neuron; involving transmissions between other  neu-
rons/receptors/in various orbits in the universe; caused by the malfunctioning of her compromised "geo chemistry" interfering with
transmissions; that  made her unwittingly vegetarian/carnivorous -as
she inadvertently attempted to  self right herself."  But, despite those
theories he did agree plants were not regenerating, and as a result was
producing less and less oxygen and edible food. As a result of examining
other theories and conclusions, "he concluded the earth was also being
smothered; and the only chance she had was the administering of B221
(and other remedies mentioned for manufacturers/consumers/an significantly involved others.)"

"Numerous 'Grid locked, do nothing government(s) not to be out-
done;  realized they were at  their wits end and had to work with other
governments/other parties of influence/the consortium /space Insti-
tute/etcetera to bring the challenging objectives to a favorable conclu-
sion – despite their previous trifling favoritism to the contrary."

# CHAPTER 8



## *Point Rubicon*

It took several years to produce this particular rather remarkable space craft (the "Witch Craft"); that incorporate many devices/ideas from the "astrotec(s);" and contributions from the Space Institute/etcetera.. Once "it" was launched there wasn't much more that could be done to ameliorate the condition(s) of mother earth; other than  man indulging in his favorite past time; being that of "Bickering over what ever." What to call it! A rocket?  a space craft?   A space vehicle?   "Or what ever!" "Otherwise, what  could be done individually or by  groups was essentially (sort) at a stand still (moot issue)."

In Some of the disenchanted groups  and organizations they could be characterized as those involved in the carbon and the pygmy man war(s)!  "The former were of the notion they wanted to use B221 in some way as the money standard (similar to the old gold standard)." "On the other hand  the pygmy men did not agree!  They were opportunistic and not too proud to accomplish their objectives with Braun or brain. "  There was also a group that was referred to as "wall streeters." "They thrived on what was referred to in the vernacular of the streets (at that time) "tec criminals!"   "There were also those as well as governments vs governments who had long since lost their way!"   But, they all talked about what could be done to fix the problem(s).  "The Solution!" Some talked about moving to another planet too. Others objected strenuously as they claimed, "considering  how we've messed this one up; we're not ready to propagate any further."

Several politicians attempted to explaining to the various factions what to expect in the future; while inept ones attempted to boldly take advantage of the opt(s); as they made remarks/speeches; boldly expressing their beliefs in the matter and  their "hate!" At such  a time, "Some would wonder if they were just suffering from ignorance, stupidity, pseudo-intellectualism, or suffering from an oppositional disorder." "Or were they just  uncivilized psycho sociaopathic psychotics-or what (egotism/genious)?"  Literally, others would say they really didn't know what was going on;  but, really loved to hear themselves talk;  takeing advantage of an impromptu media opt;  blameing others; including various  social media(s) who reported information on subject(s) in question; that may not have been true; that they swore, 'were 'fact' checked an deemed newsworthy.   But, in reality  were not true or news worthy (or helpful other than to sow more dissension and discord); an in some other instances  may have created further doubt -than utility..

*9:45 AM 3/23/2023*

"As  time for such oratory diminish  one voice being that of Pastor James Deshazer said,   "We've gotten so smart/greedy/etcetera -an now so stupid!"  "We like Dodo birds who  eventually became extinct; because they loss their ability to distinguishing who their preditors/enemies were; let alone understood why they were vulnerable; and why it could/would eventually consume them to extinction." He also  went on to explain, "comparatively speaking contributing factors of citizens  were; they have 'had' it too easy for generations  (to long -when times were good); as they  were not informed; let alone even attempted to inform them selves about such matters; did not bother to participate in the political processe(s)/ etcetera.; nor did  they trust their representatives; because they thought they did not have their interest at  heart."  Nevertheless, there was hope, "there would be a morning twilight; bringing with it a  promising outcome."     In the meantime calamities killed (so-called) good/ bad people.  Bands of thugs and outright terrorists/etcetera (in some countries) in some instances banded together; to protest and in some in-stances outright attack government assets (representatives thereof and properties); to express their displeasure.

Out of this carnage came a very interesting women's movement (if you can imagine); the idea was thought to have originated in some coun-tries/tribes of Africa (used by women); whereby their displeasures were expressed "en mass" by "Mooning;" to protest the behavior(s) of their living conditions/leaders/oppressors/chiefs/wars/etcetera. "It was one of the most effective means in their 'Tool Box;' as members from var-ious organizations on occasion(s) mooned some of the responsible ones to shame; and some subsequent action." Needless, to say none wanted moon light shining on them or their antics for long! So in some in-stances they had to concede as the light was very effective. Perhaps, you can only imagine the powerful influence(s) mood light had upon their psychic; as it encouraged their representatives/etcetera to respone to their concerns; with out the necessity of any further light (to help them see the error(s) of their way(s). Some were repulsed by the means of the moon; as it may have conjuring up thoughts of pleasure/ shame/ successes/barriers with the moon (who knows); involving them in inti-mate circumstances or otherwise; that were too personal and or taboo to share with others -and what costs.

Some of the power(s) responses were redundant reiteration(s) about how to solve the problem(s)! Some of their reiterations seemed to have influenced some characters as they remarked, "started on the right foot." "As they fumbled around for an analogy to use; it was also said, "don't forget the other foot; as this is not singularly a governmental problem alone; as human factors are not precluded." "Surely the com-ments/expressions of all totally involved; should have been enough to motivate the pros and cons (enough); to start doing what was direly needed (for the sake of all)."

"Seemingly in the end there arose many philosopher kings/poet laureates/ songwriters/ entertainers/ and so on! " They prophesied/wrote songs/entertained/wrote Poems/etcetera. Of note was a song written and performed by someone identified only as "Easy." The words of the song "Song of the Star-Spangled Banner" (see below) seemed to have had an emotionally binding patriotic influence; that bonded many of the disenchanted "groups" together.   They also came to realize her condition could be their 'swan song' too; if their work could not influence others to work together; to help diminish the challenges upon our their Mother Earth."

Song of the Star-Spangled Banner 1

I sing the Song of the Star-Spangled Banner
I sing the Song of the Star-Spangled Banner
so sing along with me
and you to shall be free
singing the Song of the Star-Spangled Banner
Star-Spangled Banner
0h,oh,oh,oh,oh
Star-Spangled Banner
Star-Spangled Banner
so sing along with me
and you two shall be free
Star-Spangled Banner
Star-Spangled Banner
0h,oh,oh,oh,oh Star-Spangled Banner


It had an emotionally binding melodic patriotic sound and effect! Maybe in the end they all sang it; in hopes that the dire conditions would all come to pass; as in a brighter future with a better understanding and outcome for their mother and themselves – her inhabitants.

"As they peered skyward from time to time; waiting on the arrival of B221 from the heavens; they watched and waited knowing; "only the future could predict the outcome." Nevertheless, they felt there was something out there; homing on its way back to Mother Earth  – that would help to ensure a favorable outcome. Soon after the positive sentiments became palpable; some other poet or song writer wrote, "There's Something Out There." It was infectious too! But, not of the magnitude of the  "Song of the Star-Spangled Banner."

There is something out there

There's something out there
we watch
we wait
we gaze
through clouds
dark nights
and sunny days
we gaze
there is something out there

*10:20 AM 3/23/2023*

The once beautiful/generous planet had stopped growing! Who could possibly say what the outcome would be; if the plant life on earth continues not to produce; and there would be Less and less oxygen; gradually smothering/starving its inhabitants. Was it all just a bad dream? When will we wake up? Trumped up rationales! Dreams to support just that!  The truth of the matter was the crew had been in space beyond the  point of expected time of return (spread unfounded doubt). With that in mind another politician also known for his oratory skills reminded them, "that their situation was  reminiscent of the predicament Rome found itself in  eons ago (The Point Of No Return)."   While another retorted reminding them,  "Rome wasn't built in a day -either."

In response it was explained,  "we are well beyond the point of no return. A point at which to turn back would definitely not be productive." "There was a consensus to proceed!"    With that in mind the president of the USA presented plans of operation for approval; as it was thought there would be some favorable  endorsement/support from Congress (who were frequently referred to by some of its citizentry/constituents  as the "4th Graders in charge.   Even with the threats of more "Moonlight;"  it was felt the balance of Congress was no longer functioning responsibly; as they appeared unable or unwilling to legislate in a responsible manner to address the dire eminent issues at hand.

The executive issued order(s) and leadership on how to proceed once the elements were harvested and brought to earth.   They were very broad and far-reaching!  They literally included all corporation(s) in the USA an its citizens/etcetera. Reluctantly, the principles of the remaining world soon followed; executing as many policies as their circumstances would allow;  that would help revitalize/restore the world! Literally, "it was as if a war had been declared -to  accomplish those ends."   There was also a reminder (from one of the speakers) that there was a plan "B!"  That being  the HR project (hobby rocket previously mentioned); that would automatically initiate in the event the mission went "south -it would go into effect."

The HR was much more sophisticated than the name implied. "It was designed to  automatically  launch; and it's avionics in  its own guidance system would home in on a prearranged beacon (signal) to guide the HR; and its precious cargo safely back to the USA on  earth." Once the spacecraft or the HR returned with samples of B221; scientifically processed (radiated) an ready for mass production an eventual distribution; it would via a previously agreed-upon plan; distributed throughout the globe; hopefully to cause regeneration soil and plant life; which in turn would produce more oxygen an food.  As the efficacy of this plan improved there would be benefits of exponential proportions.   But, there was at  least one caveat to be cognizant of!  "Even if the above mention plan  was followed;  it would take at least several years of more before there would be a  significant/promise of  a dependable harvest." Others had previouly predicted five years.  However, "for some it just did not matter an they were not comforted by their predictions.

Despite the nonbelievers/sceptics there was a unanimous collective consensus/opinion throughout  the globe; "that as humans began to un- derstand the relationship between them an his mother (he had another chance!)."   She, "Mother Earth was beginning to be seen literally as a living entity to be regarded (as a living being too); an as such had to be treated accordingly (going forward  as its inhabitants strive to build a healthy beneficial vital symbiotic  relationship with its Mother Earth).

This relationship would include modification(s) of man's behavior(s); "on his journey to becoming" a good steward of the earth; an literally becoming  the  Guardian  of  the  Universe;  or  until  his  behavior presents/determines the contrary.   This modification out of necessity would focus on solving the riddle(s) of the "gasses;" that serves literally as an "atmospheric lens" that adjust/regulate heat from sun light; thereby providing the benefits of warm life giving temperature(s) on earth an all of her dependents..   This would  not preculde further education; in- volving the further understanding  of the effects of man's contributory relationship to the riddle; that eventually lead to the vicious physical up toward symptoms; such as it's many upheavals from her bowels; an the gradual demise of plant life and the reduction of dioxide...  In the mean time they (humanity) looked forward to the arrival of B221; "that would mark the  genesis of a long journey on earth towards attainment of those lofty goals."

"Respectively, in the meantime we wait!"
END
(Their end may be just the beginning)


Out of these accounts(s) unknowingly (to be) was the birth of
'Humans' becoming
"Guardian of the universe."

www.ingramcontent.com/pod-product-compliance
Lightning Source LLC
Chambersburg PA
CBHW052235150726
48002CB00003B/1442